# Muddy Mayhem

# Muddy Mayhem

## Robin and Chris Lawrie

Illustrated by
**Robin Lawrie**

## Acknowledgements

The authors and publishers would like to thank Julia Francis, Hereford Diocesan Deaf Church lay co-chaplain, for her help with the sign language in the *Chain Gang* books.

Published by Evans Brothers Limited
2A Portman Mansions
Chiltern Street
London W1U 6NR

© Robin and Christine Lawrie
First published 2000
Reprinted 2001

Printed in Hong Kong

**British Library Cataloguing in Publication data.**
Lawrie, Robin
   Muddy Mayhem. – (The Chain Gang)
   1. Slam Duncan (Fictitious character) – Juvenile fiction
   2. All terrain cycling – Juvenile fiction 3. Adventure stories
   4. Children's stories
   I. Title II. Lawrie, Chris
   823.9'14[J]

ISBN 0 237 52105 9

Hi! My name is Duncan. My friends call me Slam. When I lived in a town, I always played football with my friends, but the truth is that I wasn't very good.

Then my Mum and Dad decided to buy a garage in the country.

On the way to our new home I wondered where you played football – there were no flat places. But it only took me a day or two to find out that everybody in my new school went . . .

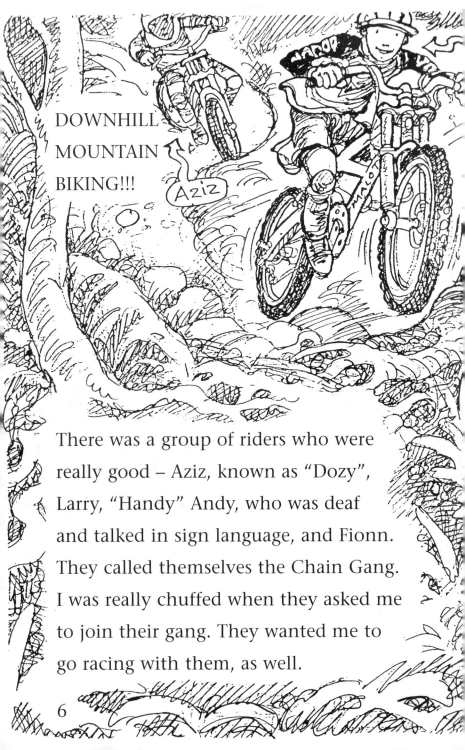

DOWNHILL
MOUNTAIN
BIKING!!!

Aziz

There was a group of riders who were
really good – Aziz, known as "Dozy",
Larry, "Handy" Andy, who was deaf
and talked in sign language, and Fionn.
They called themselves the Chain Gang.
I was really chuffed when they asked me
to join their gang. They wanted me to
go racing with them, as well.

But my old BMX wasn't really up to it.

7

The new garage didn't make much money, and a good downhill mountain bike is expensive. So one night, Dad started to build me one.

The month before, someone had sold Dad a crashed aeroplane. He thought parts of it would come in handy. The frame and all the bits were made out of a strong but light metal. Just the thing to build a bike with.

He was right, the bike was strong and light, but it wasn't very pretty, and it didn't handle well.

He also built a washing machine and a lawnmower out of it. But you could never call them beautiful, either.

Although I guess the lawnmower . . .

. . . was fast.

Sometimes I had to help my dad in the garage. I would have enjoyed this, but Dad's helpers, Spanner and Stick, were always playing tricks on me.

I thought they might be stealing from Dad when he wasn't watching, but I couldn't be sure.

When I wasn't working in the garage,
my friends and I went biking on the hill
behind my house
but my new bike
wasn't that good.

As far as we were concerned

it was our hill, until one day . . .

COOL!

B.A.C. RALLY

SPECIAL STAGE HERE Feb. 21.

BIG AIR!

*What's all this then?

11

. . . a poster was put up in the village. It said there was going to be a car rally in the area, and that next Saturday there would be a special stage on our hill. Already the village was filling up with support vehicles checking the route.

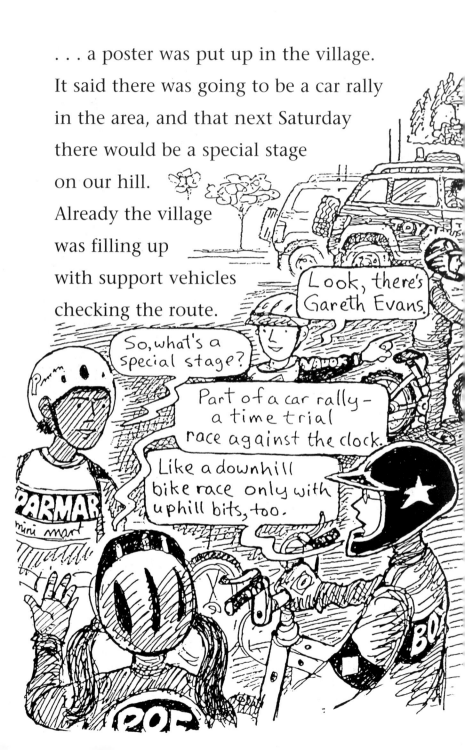

Next day another poster went up in

a local bike shop.

The hill was closed the day before the special stage, so I spent Friday afternoon helping Dad in the garage.

That evening, I was cleaning up behind the garage, when I saw Spanner and Stick in the lane nearby.

I didn't like the look of their new friend.

The next day I hardly recognized our village. All the cars were lined up for the start of the special stage. Rally leader Gareth Evans was due to go first.

It was all so exciting, I almost forgot that I had things to do.

I was too late. Spanner and Stick had thrown logs on to the road and Gareth's car was coming through the forest . . . fast!

19

Gareth saw the logs – but too late.
In half a second, the car was up to its
lights in water, with a drowned engine!

21

Gareth restarted the engine, but the cooling fan threw water back over the wires and drowned it again.

They dried the wires again and I helped push the car out of the lake.

What's the matter now? Hurry up, George!

Dropped the fan belt in the water! We'll overheat without it!

That's O.K. I'll get one from Dad's garage!

My favourite downhill course led straight back to Dad's garage.

But when I got there . . .

Then I remembered something that Dad
had told me once and I took off for home.

I knew this had to be the fastest climb
of my life, but half-way up the hill . . .

Luckily,
my favourite jump
was just around the corner
– and I could do things on my
home-made downhiller that Spanner and
Stick couldn't do on their old motorbikes!

27

Even though I had bent my frame in the massive jump I'd just done, I was back at the lake in five minutes.

The tights were tied round the pulleys.

The engine roared into life . . .

then stopped.

Before I could say anything, Gareth
had fitted the brake wire
from my bike
on to the
car's
engine.

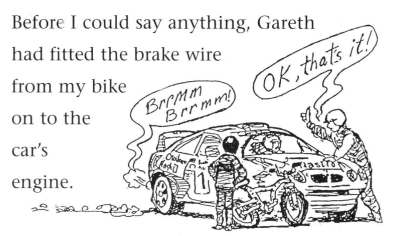

George jumped back into the car. Gareth
slammed it into gear. It lurched forward,
knocking over my bike and finishing it
off completely.

Gareth Evans blasted off up the hill.
He seemed pretty keen to make up
for lost time.

Later that night on telly . . .

Five minutes later, Dozy rang up.

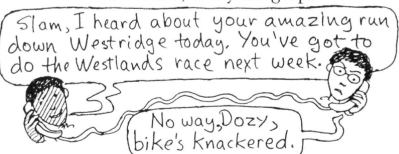

I went to bed in a pretty bad mood that night, but early next morning. . .

. . . a Team Toyaru van pulled up in front

of my house.

Two Toyaru mechanics rolled out a
beautiful, new, full-suspension,
downhill bike in
Toyaru racing
colours.

There was a note on it which said:

-To the best
mechanic
we ever had
lots of luck
-Gareth
and George

Mechanic? Forget it! I was going racing!